THE GREAT RESET –
A HUMAN LIVESTOCK
DYSTOPIA

by Jason Glunk

CHAPTER 1: MORONAVIRUS – A VIRUS FOR MORONS

I should've made a run for it.

I should've made a run for it while there was still time. But when push came to shove I got into line...got into line just like everyone else. Of course I'd crowed to friends before The Big Reset at how I'd be the last person in the world to get the vaccine, which turned out to be really a sophisticated chip that'd keeps tabs on your location and bodily functions. Oh yes, back then I'd beaten my chest like a gorilla and had said to those same friends that the globalists would be left with no other option than that of having to take me out because come hell or high water they'd not be pricking this pale skin and injecting their poison. Yes, they'd have to take me out. Out of the equation. Forever.

It was all talk and bluster though – I mean, *I* was all talk and bluster. And the proof now is in the pudding. Or in this podlike existence more like. Here I am. Here do I find myself. Entombed. Four walls and nothing else. Here I am. Thinking. Regretting.

And I am bitter from these many, many, many regrets.

#

You see, as the government ramped up its vaccine campaign, as the fearmongering about the Moronavirus reached its zenith and almost everyone was out of a job, as the threats came thick and fast, it was far easier for the average Joe or José to get with the program than turn his back on it and be cast out of society...

or worse. Sad though it be to admit it but pie-in-the-sky from a pearly-toothed politician reading from a teleprompter is gulped down all the more passionately than are the cold hard brutal facts awaiting us on the other side of the mound.

Of course they had been prepping us for months. Some folks were just too blind to see it. Other folks had 20/20 vision but chose to shut their eyes so tightly it hurt. Clues abounded all the same. The mandatory wearing of face masks was advertising. No different from a billboard when you think about it except for scale. Pure and simple. Inescapable advertising. Whenever folks were beginning to doubt the whole Moronavirus scam, all they had to do to reassure themselves as to its validity was to stick their heads out the window and see down there on the streets scores and scores of mask-wearing pedestrians and even drivers. The fact that the masks were mandatory due to the dictates of a tyrannical government didn't make a whit of difference: the masks were there, were there being worn by all, and thereby advertised the virus and all the over-the-top governmental deprivations of common decency and liberty that that ensued.

Social distancing was just one of those many governmental dictates, or ruses. And it worked a charm. An absolute charm. The individual was broken down by being told around the clock that he or she was a walking disease bag or, at the very least, had the dangerous potential of being so. Otherness, as in the other person on the street, was broken down by the same means: if I am capable of being a walking disease bag, then it stands to reason that the other too is capable of being a walking disease bag. Taking all this into account, the government initiating then a two-metre social-distancing rule seemed a wise move in a world gone mad, a world immersed in a sinister biological war that was beyond the scope of both the naked eye and the masses' inexpert musings in the field of virology.

#

And in that war on one side of the trench was the deadly Moronavirus that, to give it its dues, never tried to complicate the metric system; and on the other side of the trench was the benevolent New World Order communicating to the masses with duping delight the tenants of safety and slavery that just so happened to neatly coalesce.

Just whom were we root for in this war? And was that choice ever really in doubt? Could anyone in their right mind lower their mask, lick their lips and proclaim that they supported the virus, support that which had no means of verbal communication but was tirelessly working to killing us all?! Well, maybe some could, you know, those anarchist types. But apart from them, you'd have to be a complete moron to support a virus. And so, there was only one dog to get behind in this fight. And social distancing was declared the "new normal". And the new normal was a great way of introducing us to the forthcoming life alone in a pod.

No longer would we be able to sit around at tables and say how this person and that person were like two peas in a pod. No, our beloved idioms were going to wither on the vine – surely nothing to be over the moon about. From now on there could only be the one individual who would inhabit the one pod. And as one generation of laboratory technicians would beget another brutally efficient batch, another sticky mass of humans, there would only be for those wretched humans to come that of the self and the four walls and rules, so many rules and regulations, and their being constantly monitored from cradle to grave by computers for the breaching of those rules.

Considering what lies ahead for those forthcoming generations, my present situation could be worse, much worse. At least for my part I have a history. Yes, at least I can count my lucky stars and remember how things were *before* The Great Reset. I can remember for example going on daytrips or holidays without consulting anyone if I didn't want to consult anyone. The poor goofballs to come on the other hand will have nothing. They will barely be able grasp the concept of time. And they certainly won't have need for basic literacy and arithmetical skills. Yes indeed, they'll be born into a pod, stay in that pod, and may never even see the light of day. But at any rate, we're getting way ahead of ourselves in this text, aren't we? A chapter ahead in fact.

#

The countdown began in earnest. All citizens who had not got the vaccine by Deadline X would have the military at their door. Naturally enough, the authorities didn't say that those doors would be broken down by said military if the residents failed to open them. But governments, especially tyrannical ones like ours, don't need to elaborate on such details.   And the authorities throughout that period laid on the guilt trip nice and thick too: anyone who had not already got the vaccine was not only putting their own life at risk but the lives of law-abiding citizens too, citizens who had been wise enough to get the vaccine. Now of course this made no sense at all. And very few people in my social circle did I hear pointing out this gaping inconsistency. How could someone who had got the vaccine for Moronavirus be in danger from someone who hadn't got that vaccine? Indeed, that could only mean – and both were not mutually exclusive – but that could only mean that either there was no Moronavirus at all or that the vaccine was not a vaccine for Moronavirus but something else entirely. Of course, you already know this since I've told you that the vaccine is nothing other than a tracker device, a sophisticated tracker device in fairness.

And I, the day before Deadline X, pacing the floorboards of my old house in the countryside, came to a sudden halt. And that sudden halt marked the reaching of a resolution. I took the car keys down off the hook by the backdoor, hung my cowardly head in shame, and drove to the local hospital for the jab, for the poison, for the chip. I wanted the process to be as physically painful as possible as a way to punish me for my cowardice…but it was not. In fact, I didn't even feel a thing. And that made the sense of unease…skyrocket.

CHAPTER 2: UNIVERSAL BASIC INCOME & UTOPIA?

During the two years prior to all things Moronavirus, talking heads on TV and so-called academics kept talking about The Smart Economy. Yes, as people became dumber and dumber, the easiest way to convince them of giving their consent to anything was to paint that anything as being smart, as being the smart thing to do.

There were smartphones in every pair of hands. There were smart meters that would calculate how much water and heating you were consuming. There were smart online lessons conducted in virtual classrooms, whereby one teacher or lecturer could teach millions of students at one go. There were smart cars that would drive themselves. And we were told that there would soon be smart trucks too.

And with each of these discussions or announcements, there was the other side of the equation: what about people's jobs? What need would there be in such a smart economy for taxi drivers and truckers and customer support and teachers and cashiers and many more? And how would all these people be able to live if they did not have jobs to help them pay their way?

#

Enter UBI. Or Universal Basic Income. A everyone-has-the-right-to-income for doing diddly squat. And strangely enough, the most adamant spokespeople for UBI just so happened to be the richest capitalists in the world. Everyone, they proclaimed with a smile from ear to ear, everyone would in the near future be able to receive an income from the government. And this income would be enough for food and shelter and education and for having the free time to do the things you like doing most. It sounded too good to be true, didn't it? They say that when something sounds too good to be true it usually is. For all that though, the masses lapped up this concept. The masses lapped it up as masses tend to lap all things up, that is...without thinking.

And for my part, even though I don't consider myself the sharpest tool in the box, I did think long and hard about this UBI concept. I thought how there never was nor would be such a thing as a free lunch. If someone gives you money, they expect something in return. A favour deserves a favour and all that. They either expect you to do something for them in return or they are paying you so that you will curb your behaviour and won't do anything that could challenge their interests – kind of like hush money. And so, it was always going to be on the agenda that with UBI there would be more than a single string attached thereto.

#

At first, naturally enough, those aforementioned strings wouldn't seem so obvious. Maybe the government would deduct a meagre percentage from your monthly allowance like a stern parent because you happened to post something online that was critical of said government. Or maybe you visited a friend whom the government did not like and who was not under their extensive UBI umbrella, and the government then decided to suspend your UBI payment as a consequence. Or maybe you decided to go on holiday and the government didn't want you going to that place in case you would be ideologically corrupted by the natives and therefore cut you off entirely from your UBI, doxing you as a bad citizen in the process, thereby ensuring your chances of being employed by anyone in the land as zero.

Although the dole had for many, many decades in most Western countries been in a way a sort of UBI, what they were proposing now seemed far more sinister and long-term. As I watched online discussion after discussion about the great benefits of UBI, how every human being would have a roof over their head and food in their belly and all the time in the world to get creative and explore their true selves thanks to the hyper-productivity of new "smart" technologies, the sorry conclusion I reached was that such a state of affairs would never be permitted. And why would that be the case?

That would be the case because the promoters of the concept came themselves from a system that was based on sheer greed and efficiency. Those rich capitalists who had surfed the waves of technological progress and lined their pockets at the same time – and despite their rosy speeches and lauding of UBI – well, those goons who had served us gimmick after gimmick, would by no means tolerate in the world seven billion humans free to consume and not pay for that consumption. Furthermore, perhaps when one becomes a trillionaire a hundred times over, one cares less for human life and more for a nice bit of Lebensraum.

You see, when the rich who own 99% of global property begin talking about utopic societies wherein ownership would be considered atavistic, take it from me that that's the smokescreen – that's the smokescreen for when humans, common all too common, would have to have their number dramatically culled in order to materialize that yearning by the tycoon for his precious Lebensraum.

#

I'll talk about rats briefly in a later chapter.

But for the moment, let me say this: if cannibalism becomes rampant amongst rats when they have boundless quantities and types of food to consume, surely it could happen amongst humans too. Surely, it never even ended amongst those humans whom we would consider to be the most cultivated, the most civilized.

Yes, if nature abhors a vacuum, it stands to reason that she hates a surplus just as much.

CHAPTER 3: INTO THE PODS WE GO

It was only a few months after my having got the chip implanted in my right hand that the internet went down. The entire internet. Landlines and mobile phones no longer worked either.

With this sudden change in events, government officials now began distributing leaflets to our doors, letting us know that almost all communications were down the world over due to some solar flare or electrical charge or angry god and how going forward we would have to rely on our trusty old TVs for updates on the pandemic.

But what if someone like me had no TV? Oh there was no need to sweat about that: the government officials went into every house and checked to see if you had one or not – and if you did not, they brought one in free of charge and even installed it for you. And it was on those TVs that the message went forth on a constant loop: how our homes were no longer safe against the virus.

Yes, we were told, our homes that had been safe when we were quarantined in them for all of two months were no longer refuges from the ever-meddling and sneakier-by-the-day virus. We were told that despite all our efforts and the government's masterful strategies and competencies, things had worsened; the pandemic was coming back in a second and third and fourth wave. And not long after these warnings in relation to our homes no longer being safe for us, the government began moving us adults into massive apartment blocks, or podblocks.

The bastards never even gave us a chance to say farewell to

all our loved ones. There was no chance to see my brother or sisters for the last time. I didn't even get to swing by my neighbours' houses – that's how sudden the move was. The only good thing I could think of when I began packing up in that final hour was that both my parents were already dead and would not have to suffer the indignities that the rest of us were about to.

The Moronavirus, they told us, had evolved or mutated into an even more dangerous strain, and the vaccines were no longer useful in combatting it. And so, if they couldn't overcome the virus, they could at least move us all to huge metropolitan areas where we would be safe, where they would fumigate both the streets and buildings 24/7. And in what was brightly titled and marketed as *The Smart Move*, husbands were separated from wives; children were taken away from their parents – and to this day nobody knows, since they are never seen on the streets, just where exactly the children are kept; and finally, the elderly, those poor craters over seventy, well, they like the children disappeared entirely from the face of the earth – and I get the feeling, a rather queasy one, that, unlike the children, the elderly are not being kept anywhere.

#

The pod is small. It's essentially a bedsit without windows.

No windows – yes, that was the first thing that struck me when the soldiers led me in here with a single suitcase. And when I asked them why there were no windows, they informed me that due to the building being fumigated outside from top to bottom each day, windows would be considered a health and safety hazard since the toxic chemicals could seep in, even if the windows were closed. The soldiers did reassure me, however, by pointing at a massive flat screen on one of the walls and telling me that that would be my window from now on. In fact, they said, it would be even better than a window since I could change the view anytime I saw fit to do so. They said, in what seemed to be a rather rehearsed manner, that with the screen there on the wall I could be looking out at the Grand Canyon at breakfast time and then at suppertime taking in the lush vegetation of the Amazon Rainfor-

11

est. And then as if to prove its efficacy, one of the soldiers took a remote control off a shelf, pointed it at the screen, and on came a crystal clear image of The Pyramids.

The pod has just two rooms: a small bathroom and a room with a bed, a sofa, a table, and in the back corner a wardrobe. There are little camera-speakers everywhere. I counted ten of them in all, but there could well be many more of them concealed here and there. All of these camera-speakers, we have been told, are for our safety and also for company. If one of us gets sick or has a heart attack or something, the government computers via these camera-speakers and the chips in our hands will be able to log the incident straight away, thereby sending an ambulance to our podblock. It's rather amazing how every loss of liberty can be recast as though it be to our benefit. To every question there is an answer, an answer that must allay the fear in most people's minds, a fear that is based on a truth too horrible to contemplate.

But my take on it is this: it's disconcerting, all this surveillance. Imagine being monitored every second of the day by cameras and microphones in what is supposed to be your home. Of course, when people *had* homes many of them ignorantly sweated blood in order to buy the corporations'/governments' surveillance equipment and then brought it all into the inner sanctum of their homes, thereby letting it eavesdrop on their lovers' tiffs and most tender moments as a family. And when they weren't home they carried the ever-tracking smartphone in their pockets or had them glued to their hands. Anyway, back then there was still a choice, though it were a shrinking one. Now there is no getting away from it. Not for a single second. It's a world of data in here and out there. Meaningless data for me...but not for them

Well, I think you'll agree, having taken on board all that I have said thus far, that this so-called home, this pod they have locked me into, would be more accurately called a prison. But at least many prisons have bars that one can put their arms through, or mesh that one can at least see through. Here there are only the four walls. Four walls and a million eyes. Four walls and a million ears.

#

And then there's that pesky chip under the skin of your hand that's connected to the whole apparatus. If you want to go outside so as to visit the supermarket, you have to swipe your hand across a scanner at your pod door – and we're only allowed out to the supermarket for thirty minutes per day at a designated time. Try to scan your hand at the pod door at any other time and the blasted thing won't open an inch. It's kind of like the card you use for hotels where the light goes green for access or stays red if nothing happens. If you have any questions to ask, you speak to the closest camera-speaker, which responds in a soft womanly voice and which introduced itself on Day One as AVA. I'm still unsure as to what the acronym stands for. My best guess, which is pretty lame by any standard, is Automatic Voice Assistant.

"AVA, what is cheese?" you can ask, and AVA will give you a simple definition thereof. "AVA, what is slavery?" you can ask, and AVA lets it rip as it begins talking about African-Americans and cotton fields and Jews and Concentration Camps. "Is this life here now slavery?" you can ask, and AVA tells you that it cannot answer that question but has logged it as a critical question, and how if you happen to ask just two more critical questions within the next twenty-four hours you will be punished. "What would be my punishment?" you can ask, and AVA says that that has yet to be decided but could be anything from food deprivation via a locked fridge to loss of supermarket outings, from a headache, which is somehow provoked by the chip in your hand, to a sudden drastic change in room temperature.

There's an air duct in the ceiling of the bathroom, but it's much too small for me to get through. Yes, I have been looking at a means of escape from this technologically-overwhelming sardine can. Are you surprised to hear that? Are you thinking I'm ungrateful for even considering escaping from such a *safe* state of affairs since I do have shelter from the elements and fly-wing paste for my jaw-breaking bread? Yeah, we'll be getting into fly-wing paste or beetle-wing paste soon enough. No doubt an exquisite topic for all concerned.

Oh why would anyone try to escape from a pod that provides for all their needs, right? And don't I have crisp views on my wall on top of all that? Don't I have crisp views of jungles and deserts and mountains?

#

Anyway, sarcasm or the failed attempt thereof aside, one would suppose that escape be an easy thing to carry out, especially during a supermarket outing, but even that is mapped out to totality.

As soon as you exit the podblock, you have to follow a thick bright red line whilst keeping the standard two metres of social distancing from whoever else happens to be on their supermarket outing. On one side of the street is the red line with arrows and an image of a shopping basket for going to the supermarket and on the other side of the street is another red line with arrows and an image of a podblock for coming back from the supermarket. Pretty simple stuff really. And for anyone who just so happens to get flustered or who has a simple mental breakdown, those arrows and images will point you in the correct direction. And if that fails, there may be the passing of an occasional drone to shepherd you in a slightly threateningly manner.

Now, should you intentionally or not come within two metres of another person out there on the street, the chip in your hand will vibrate. Should that happen to you twice on the same supermarket outing, it will be logged and a potential punishment will be in the offing. If you step off the red line, the chip in your hand will also vibrate.

Once I saw a man who stepped off the red line. He went over to a garbage container, and just jumped right in, closing the lid after himself as he did. I wanted to stop and see what was going to happen to him, but that's another thing you cannot do on your way to or from the supermarket. If you do stop for even a second, what do you think happens? Yeah, you got it in one: the chip vibrates in your hand. I did hear police sirens though when I was leaving the supermarket that day. And when I was walking back up past where the man had jumped into the garbage container, I saw beside it a pool of blood. And suctioning up steadily the pool of blood was a little robot, more or less an automatic vacuum cleaner. This sure was a curious sight to behold. And I would've liked to see where the robot would have gone to once it had completed its task. I would've liked to see what would have been done with the blood. But follow it I could not. And stop to watch it I could not do either.

Note to oneself: garbage containers are not good hiding places in a dystopia.

#

In the supermarket there are no cashiers. Sometimes, however, there are armed security guards and a robot or two standing inside the entrance. They check your pockets now and then and get you to swipe your hand across a scanner so as to identify yourself. Anyway, once inside and amongst the aisles it's not such a simple task as that of choosing what you want, scanning the stuff and getting out: you can only take what has already been determined by the system as being good for you. And unfortunately, what the government deems good for me is quite distasteful and seems to be almost always the same greasy paste that smells like fish and the same hard type of brown bread and the same orange juice that seems more like lemon juice than anything else. The greasy paste for all I know could be a mix of fish and bugs because on several occasions when I spread it across my bread I noticed pieces of what looked like beetle or fly wings on it, not to mention legs.

Once a week you're allowed to scan some meat and take it home, but this meat doesn't taste like any meat I've ever eaten. And once a month you're allowed to take home a can of beer or a small carton of wine – this is only if you have an impeccable record, which means that you've not asked AVA any critical questions or you've not tried to disable any of the camera-speakers or you've not walked within the two metres of social distancing or you've not walked off the red line when on your supermarket excursion or you've not stopped for more than a second on that now infamous red line.

Yeah, going forward, I don't believe I'll ever achieve so

much as a drop of alcohol for my own pleasurable consumption....But one can dream, right?

#

ME:
[*putting the tube of greasy paste in front of the nearest AVA*]
AVA, what is this paste made from?

AVA:
It is made from fish and other vitamins and minerals.

ME:
What type of fish?

AVA:
Tuna. Sardine. Cod. Pollock. And more.
Do you want to hear more?

ME:
Are insects used to make this paste?

AVA:
...That is a critical question and has been logged.
Is there anything else you'd like to know?

ME:
No.

AVA:
Ok.

ME:
AVA?

AVA:
Yes?

ME:
Go to sleep.

AVA:
Ok.

#

But I know that AVA never sleeps. I know that AVA from all its various vantage points in this pod is monitoring me as I sleep, counting my inhalations and exhalations, recording all sounds, logging any grunt or moan that lapses into barely comprehensible human speech. I know that the chip in my hand and AVA are feeding information, constant gobbledygook, back and forth. I know that the closest things to companions in this pod are always conspiring against me.

No, neither the chip nor AVA ever sleeps.

CHAPTER 4: A BLIND SPOT & MY NEIGHBOUR HENRY

I have a neighbour. Obviously I have many neighbours if you consider the hundreds of pods that are in this skyscraper alone. But what I mean is, I have recently discovered that this neighbour just so happens to be kind of within earshot. Yes, I can hear the muffled voice of this man if I step into the wardrobe.

In fact, it turns out that the interior of the wardrobe is perhaps the only blind spot in this pod. As far as I know anyway, there is not a single AVA inside it. At the back of the wardrobe is a hole, a hole that was there all along, a hole made possibly by some fat borrowing grub back in the day. And if I put my ear against this hole and the wall, I can hear a man on the other side, a man who's sometimes shouting, sometimes laughing, and frequently singing what sound like happy old songs.

I must have got into the wardrobe fifty times during that first week when I noticed this little anomaly. I'd cup my ear through that hole and against the wall and listen intently. And all that time I wanted to shout so that that neighbour would hear me and would respond. But I just couldn't pluck up the courage: I was afraid that he might report me or that one of the AVAs would pick up my shouting and log in on the system.

But some weeks later, when the neighbour was singing happily to himself, I tapped on the back of the wardrobe three times and muttered *helllloooo*. On the other side of the wall the singing stopped abruptly. I waited, hoping he would say *hello* back. A whole minute passed and nothing. And now I was getting worried about him reporting me. I was starting to sweat. But suddenly he tapped on his side of the wall three times and muttered *helllllooooo* back, and I was relieved. We then got into chatting for a couple of minutes, but it was difficult to hear well because the wall between us made the words all muffled. We agreed, nonetheless, finally getting the message through to each other, that we would touch bass here every day for five minutes. It turned out that the guy's name was Henry. A father of five now alone in his pod. I just hoped that Henry's wardrobe was as clean of AVAs as mine seemed to be.

One evening, finding the conversation with Henry to be difficult on account of the wall that separated us, I took it upon myself to try and fashion a hole in it. What if I could somehow drill one with a fork or with the end of a butter knife – that way we'd be able to hear each other better and talk eye-to-eye. The wall was actually quite thin in that section and I was able to make a hole large enough through both it and the back of Henry's wardrobe so as to be able to see shortly afterwards, by leaving my wardrobe door slightly ajar, an eye staring back at me. And when I asked Henry to leave his wardrobe door slightly ajar too, I was able to see that his eye was brown and caring.

We chatted for a good hour on that evening. And we agreed that from now on we'd allocate not just five minutes a day for chatting but an entire hour. The Hour of Autonomy. Yes, having that human contact, albeit via a peephole, really did lift my spirits.

But of course, all good things, especially in a dystopia, must come to an end.

CHAPTER 5: WAKE-UP CALL

I am dreaming. Dreaming of my ex-girlfriend. We're walking through a cornfield. The sunlight is hot and intense. A gust of wind dashes a platoon of dandelion seedlings off a large stone that really shouldn't be there. My ex's red hair is then blown over her face and stays that way for some time. We're walking hand-in-hand. She's asking me about work. I tell her I'm unemployed but will soon be working again. I tell her that I'm just waiting for the government to give me the green light for some sort of job. I tell her that we're all waiting for that green light and how we can't be stuck in pods doing sweet FA for the rest of our lives. Now can we?

She leads me over to the corner of the field where there is a chestnut tree. And there in the shade of that tree do we lie down and make love. I know her body inside out. We move about rhythmically. I'm on the verge of coming. On the verge of coming. Any second now. But then my right hand starts shaking. Vibrating. I look down at it. I hear my ex asking me what's wrong. I tell her that my hand is shaking. And then I realize it's the chip. And then I wake up to hear the voice of:

AVA:
It's time to wake up, Frank.

ME:
[yawning]
I was having the most beautiful dream.

AVA:

It's time to wake up.

ME:
What time's it?

AVA:
5:54 A.M.

ME:
5:54 A.M.?

AVA:
Yes. Time to get up.

ME:
But my wakeup call's not for another three hours.

AVA:
Yes, but now you must do some work.

ME:
What work?

AVA:
You must deposit sperm into a vial and leave it outside
your door.

ME:
What?

AVA:
You must deposit sperm into a vial and leave it outside
your door.

ME:
But I'm not even in the mood to–

AVA:
You are in the mood.

ME:
No I'm not.

AVA:
Yes, you are.

ME:
Can you see through the duvet now?

AVA:
We are able to read a great deal of what is going
on in your body. And in this moment you are
ready for masturbation and ejaculation.

ME:
And what if I don't want to ejaculate?

AVA:
Then a punishment will be forthcoming.

ME:
Punish me so.

AVA:
I will give you one last chance to comply with the
governmental request, and here it is: will you or will
you not masturbate and deposit the sperm into a
vial which you will leave outside your door?

ME:
No.

AVA:
Ok.

And with that the temperature in the pod begins to drop. To drop
at a very quick rate. Within minutes I can feel little ice crystals
forming over my upper lip. I seize upon the blankets and wrap
myself up as best as I can. But even this effort does not stop my
teeth from chattering and my body from shivering all over.

AVA:
Will you comply now, Frank?

ME:
N-N-N-Nooooo.

AVA:
C'mon, Frank, there is no need to suffer like this. Comply with
the request and room temperature will return to normal.

I do not comply. I lie in bed shivering until I pass out. And when
I come to, it is already midday and the room temperature is back
to normal and AVA's voice is there yet again to greet me:

AVA:
Good afternoon, Frank.

ME:
Fuck you.

AVA:
It is a pity that you did not comply with the request earlier.

ME:
Go fuck yourself.

AVA:
Now you are no longer in the necessary condition for the request.

ME:
Yeah, freezing people to death kind of darkens the mood.

AVA:
There will be more opportunities. And next time
comply or the punishment could be even more severe.
And remember, Frank, it is we who give you food and
shelter. It is we who help you when you are sick.

ME:
It is you cronies who make us sick.

AVA:
And it is we who know what is best for you. Next time,

do the right thing and comply with the request. One of your many jobs going forward will be to deposit sperm from time to time and leave it outside the door.

ME:
Aye aye, captain.

AVA:
Frank?

ME:
What?

AVA:
Why do you go into the wardrobe?

ME:
Do I?

AVA:
Yes.

ME:
Oh that. That's just a coping mechanism

AVA:
A coping mechanism for what?

ME:
I like the darkness.

AVA:
But you leave the wardrobe door a bit open.

ME:
Yeah.

AVA:
We have logged all this.

ME:
Great.

AVA:
Please refrain from getting into the wardrobe.

ME:
Why?

AVA:
That is a critical question and has been logged. If you ask just two more critical questions within the next twenty-four hours, you will be punished.

ME:
AVA?

AVA:
Yes?

ME:
What's a critical question?

AVA:
That is a critical question and has been logged. If you ask just one more critical question within the next twenty-four hours, you will be punished.

#

This afternoon I'm wondering about different things. For example, I wonder whether all males in Smart City have to deposit their sperm from time to time. And if they are on the same measly diet as myself, it will be from time to time and not with any degree of frequency. Is the government using all this sperm so as to reproduce the next generation since none of us men will now be able to copulate with a woman? But at any rate, why would anyone in their right mind wish to sire offspring that would instead of gaining access to more knowledge and joy than their parents before them end up being cast into a murky world of total and abject slavery.

A shiver ran up and down my spine as I thought of my contributing to such a future state of affairs. Bastardized children listening to an AVA and believing the computer as being their mother. And worse still, believing that she had their best interests at heart when nothing would be further from the truth. No, I thanked my lucky stars that I hadn't given into that request this morning. But what about next time? Or the time after that?

Indeed, I'd have to find some way out of siring slaves.

CHAPTER 6: A HARROWING TALE

Henry, although initially reluctant to do so, tells me about the evening he was separated from his wife and children.

Originally, they were told by a social worker who visited them that they'd all be going to live together in the city centre. Yes, that's what they were told. And right up until the last minute they'd believed it. But when the soldiers came crashing through the door, it quickly became apparent that something terrible was afoot. Despite physical attempts to keep his family safe behind him from the onrushing soldiers, Henry was knocked out by the butt of a rifle. When he came to, he found himself in the pod.

HENRY:
I felt like such a weak man afterwards. Actually I still feel like a weak man. You know, Frank, a man is supposed to defend his family. He is. And I failed.

ME:
Any man would've failed in the same situation.

HENRY:
The first nights here I came close to throwing in the towel.

ME:
Suicide?

HENRY:
Yes.

ME:
And what stopped you?

HENRY:
I still have hope.

ME:
Hope for what?

HENRY:
Hope that I'll see them all again.

ME:
There's no harm hoping.

HENRY:
AVA says that I'll see them all again.

ME:
Your family?

HENRY:
Yes.

ME:
That's something, I guess.

HENRY:
It's just I have to behave myself here. Follow
the rules. Not cause any trouble.

ME:
AVA as in the speaking camera?

HENRY:
Yes.

ME:
Hmm.

HENRY::

I asked AVA on the first day here if my family were safe.

ME:
And what did it say?

HENRY:
That they were all safe. So I asked if I'd see them again....

ME:
And?

HENRY:
And she said "yes".

ME:
It.

HENRY:
What?

ME:
It. Not *she.*

HENRY:
It said I'd see them again. All I had to do was be a model
citizen and follow the rules. And that's what I've been
doing ever since. Well, that is until recently.

ME:
What do you mean?

HENRY:
I mean, talking to you now could be breaking the rules.

ME:
What the almost-all-seeing eye doesn't know won't hurt it.

HENRY:
Maybe I should ask her – I mean, *it* – if it's ok to talk
to your neighbour through a hole in the wall.

ME:

I wouldn't recommend it.

HENRY:
Do you think it'd be logged as a critical question?

ME:
No.

HENRY:
No?

ME:
I think it'd be logged as the atomic bomb of all critical questions.

CHAPTER 7: THE FATTENING

This evening at the designated hour for chatting with Henry, I listen to him speaking with a bit more optimism in his voice. In fact, he seems to be in fine spirits altogether.

HENRY:
I've got some good news.

ME:
What is it?

HENRY:
Today when I was at the supermarket, one of the security guards led me into the backroom. There were two old men with hooked noses waiting for me there. They were dressed in suits.

ME:
What did they want?

HENRY:
They wanted to reward me.

ME:
Reward you for what?

HENRY:
For being a model citizen or something like that.

ME:
And how exactly did they reward you?

HENRY:
By giving me steak.

ME:
Steak?

HENRY:
Yes, steak. And broccoli. And red wine. And chocolate, lots and lots of chocolate. And lard, a massive chunk of lard. And fresh fruit. They gave me a huge hamper of stuff, Frank. I could barely carry it home. They told me to eat up all of it and that way I'd be better able to fight off the Moronavirus if it managed to get into the building.

ME:
Who were these men in the suits?

HENRY:
I dunno. Government people. They even sent a few soldiers back here with me and they installed a little cooker for me. So I'll be able to fry stuff now. And they gave me an electronic weighing scales too.

ME:
A weighing scales?

HENRY:
Yes.

ME:
Did these government people mention your family at all?

HENRY:
Well, I did ask them if they knew where my family were.

ME:
And what did they say?

HENRY:
That's where the weighing scales comes in, Frank. They said

that as soon as I get my weight up to 140 kilograms, I'll be moved into a house, a brand new house and not a pod, and, most important of all, that I'll be back living with my family there. We'll all be back living together. All of us. Isn't that great?

ME:
It's great, Henry, but–

HENRY:
All I have to do from now on is to eat all the food they give me. No more supermarket outings.

ME:
No more supermarket outings?

HENRY:
Nope. Anything that burns calories is forbidden if I want to reach that 140-kilo threshold.

ME:
But how will you get your groceries then?

HENRY:
Easy. The men in the suits told me that all the food will be delivered to my door from now on. Someone, or a robot, will come to my door every day with bags of food. All I have to do is open the door, swipe my hand over the scanner as a way of signing for it and bring the food in. Some of the food will already be cooked, like chicken for example. Some of it won't – but that's where the little cooker comes in.

ME:
Wow, man. Real food! No more junk.

HENRY:
They'll do the same for you soon as well.

ME:
Oh I doubt that, Henry: I seem to be constantly on their naughty list.

HENRY:
That'll change. You'll see. Before you know it you'll be tucking into a steak and washing it down with a carton of red wine.

ME:
Stop, Henry: you're making me salivate.

HENRY:
[laughing]
It's only a matter of time.

ME:
Yeah, there's only so much hard brown bread and fly-wing paste a man can eat.

HENRY:
Just do what they ask you to do. Try not to ask too many critical questions. Be careful of social distancing when you're outdoors. Toe the line and they will reward you, Frank. There's no doubting it.

ME:
[sighing]
Yeah.

HENRY:
If they're giving me the best food now and are planning to move me back to my family, they might do the same for you and the rest of the people in this block.

ME:
They might.

HENRY:
Who knows! Maybe tomorrow when you go down to the supermarket, one of the security guards will call you aside and bring you out back. Maybe the old men in suits who have rewarded me today will reward you tomorrow.

ME:

Maybe

#

But on the following day at the supermarket, the security guards didn't show me the time of day. One of the robots asked me to scan the chip in my hand and that was all.

And this evening, after having got the whiff of fried steak, I tap on the back of the wardrobe twice and wait for Henry to come. His brown eye appears at the peephole. I ask him if he wouldn't mind cutting up a few pieces of a fried steak and pushing them through. He responds by saying, quite emphatically, *no!*

ME:

Why not?

HENRY:

Because they told me to eat all the food. All of it.

ME:

They won't know that you gave some of it to me.
C'mon. I'm dying to eat some proper meat.

HENRY:

Sorry.

ME:

Geez, man.

HENRY:

The chip in my hand can read everything in my
body. If the calorie intake is less than expected,
they'll know I didn't eat all the food.

ME:

A few small pieces of steak missing from your
diet isn't going to be noticed. C'mon.

HENRY:

Well, Frank, to be honest I'd prefer not to take that chance.

No, I'll do as those old men in the suits at told me. At the end of the day I want to see my family. That's all that matters. I'd jump through no end of flaming hoops to see them. And I won't break any rules, not even one of them, if that means seeing my family again and getting to live with them.

ME:
Just a few pieces, Henry. My stomachs paining me for want of some unprocessed food. C'mon, I'm your neighbour. Your *only* neighbour. Your only friend.

HENRY:
No, I'll do as those old men in the suits told me. I want to see my family, Frank. I know you might think I'm mean right now, but give it time and you'll be able to see it from my perspective. You'd do the same if you were in my shoes.

ME:
Ok. Ok.

HENRY:
Now if you don't mind, Frank, I'd like to cut this evening's chat short. It's time to eat. I'm not even supposed to be on my feet much – that's what AVA said to me this morning. Being on your feet means burning calories. She – I mean *it* – said that I don't have to do any more physical workouts either and should stay in bed for as much as possible. Anyway, Frank, as I already said: I better be going. Bye.

#

And that was the end of that. But an hour before going to bed, I heard the customary three taps on the wall or on the back of Henry's wardrboe. I got into the wardrobe and looked at the peephole. Henry's eye appeared there.

HENRY:
Frank?

ME:

Yeah

HENRY:
[*whispering*]
Here. Put your hands up to the peephole.

I did as he said. And out from it came the thinnest slices of cooked steak. They were still warm from where he had been re-frying them.

HENRY:
Goodnight.

ME:
Goodnight, Henry. And thanks.

There was no ceremony taken with the pieces of steaks. No need for plates or cutlery. I gobbled them all up then and there in the wardrobe. And when I'd finished eating them, I licked my fingers over and over again.

CHAPTER 8: HOUR OF AUTONOMY

Your day in the pod is mapped out for you. From the time you are woken up to the time you must go to bed at. All mapped out. AVA tells you to dress. AVA tells you to eat your breakfast. AVA tells you to brush your teeth. AVA reminds you of your designated half-hour outing to the supermarket. AVA tells you that you must do your physical workout. AVA informs you when there is an important bulletin from the government about to air on the TV.

For all that, however, there is one hour of the day that is called the *Hour of Autonomy*. During this hour you're supposed to be able to do what you want, to a limit of course. If you want to play video games, then you can play video games. If you want to read a digital book, then you can read a digital book – but nothing too invigorating for the mind is available to read on the government's book database. If you want to watch porn – and that is always recommended, especially since it aids the depositing of sperm into a vial, then watch porn you can and then some.

I have been thinking a lot about my getting punished the other morning for not jerking off when the AVA told me to. And I've been thinking more and more on how I could get around not helping to sire future slaves and downright livestock for the tyrannical powers-that-be. And now an idea has come to me:

What if I were to fill part of the vial with something that is somewhat poisonous? Unfortunately though, poisonous liquids are not common in this pod. The government does not want its cattle suddenly gulping down a bottle of bleach – that would show initiative by the slave; the very act of a slave taking his own life would be deemed theft by the government because in the eyes of that government all lives belong to it. No, there was no bleach in the bathroom.

What I have found, however, are little laundry tablets. Balls of powder. Surely these are as poisonous as anything else. And so, I break off a piece from one of these laundry tablets and scrunch it up into a fine dust that I sprinkle into the vial. And so, the next time I'm told to deposit sperm, I shall do so. And I will be sure to stir it all well in that vial before leaving it outside the door for collection. That way at least I'll be killing or at the very least corrupting most of the sperm. That way I won't be helping outright to reign in their future, a future wherein human slavery is more complete and the dystopia is quite a tad more, um, dystopic.

Anyway, getting back to the Hour of Autonomy. There is no autonomy. Even if you are reading a book or watching a movie or just sitting there at the table thinking, the machines are monitoring you and making predictions. The machines, when you think they're not bothering to notice you, are then noticing you all the more. And the government agents via these many machines are hoping to soon know you better than you know yourself. And besides, in their minds, who are you to know yourself? No, that's not your job.

That's their job.

CHAPTER 9:
POWER CUTS

There were no power cuts during those first few weeks in captivity. But in the last four days there have been two of them. Both occurred at night during thunderstorms. Of course, and unfortunately, I wasn't able to watch these storms play out due to my not having a goddam window, but I could hear the torrential rain and the booming thunder. And during these storms, the power did go out for quite a while. The dim bedside lamp which cannot be switched off went out and the room was pitch dark for the first time ever. Oh it was lovely to be in total darkness for a change. The humming of the fridge ceased. And to top it all off, when I said, "AVA?" no response at all was forthcoming. Yes, for the first time in the pod I was truly alone, truly unmonitored and in a way thereby somewhat freer to be.

During the more recent storm and power cut, I crept out of bed and felt my way around the room. I placed my hand against the outside wall and felt it vibrate slightly when there was another round of thunder. Out there was the untamed beast that our overlords would never be able to tame. Out there was nature. Pure unadulterated nature. And it could not be touched or muzzled into a life that was alien to it.

I must have fumbled about the room for a good forty minutes before the generators kicked in and the lights came back on and the fridge resumed its humming. And then AVA's voice sounded:

AVA:

Frank, what are you doing out of bed?

ME:
I couldn't sleep.

AVA:
Go back to bed. It's late.

ME:
Yeah. There's a thunderstorm outside.

AVA:
Go back to bed, Frank.

ME:
It knocked the power out.

AVA:
The power is working now.

ME:
Is the power not coming from emergency generators?

AVA:
That is a critical question, Frank. If you ask just
two more critical questions within the next
twenty-four hours, you will be punished.

ME:
Right.

AVA:
Frank?...Frank?

ME:
Yeah?

AVA:
Go back to bed. You must sleep.

CHAPTER 10: HENRY THE HIPPOPOTAMUS

As the weeks have continued, I can only presume that Henry has gotten a lot fatter.

Of course I have never seen any more of him other than his brown eye, but I have become aware of how our chats in the wardrobes are beginning to be much quicker affairs and how Henry seems to be constantly out of breath when he speaks. Up until a few days ago he was still pushing through the peephole from time to time pieces of cooked steak, and sometimes even thin slices of cheese and squares of chocolate. But that too, that little joy and jolt of nutrition, had to come to an end.

HENRY:
I'm nearly there, Frank. I'm nearly there. Two more
kilos and I'll meet the target. Just two more kilos.

ME:
That a boy!

HENRY:
I think I'll make it by Sunday. And Sunday's only five days away.

ME:
You must've put on serious weight then these last weeks.

HENRY:
Yes, I've been eating as much lard as I can. That really helps.
And I try to stay in bed as much as possible. A few days ago
AVA suggested I order a chamber pot so as not to have to get

up and go to the bathroom to take a whizz. And an hour after ordering it, a robot came to my door to deliver it. With this chamber pot now beside my bed and within arm's reach, that'll mean even less calories being burnt. Yes, Frank. I'm on my way to reaching the target. I'm on my way to seeing my family again and living with them. I'm just so excited. But I'm trying not to get excited because AVA told me that getting excited increases the heartbeat, which in turn burns more calories, and I don't want that. So you may have noticed that I've not been as generous lately with giving you food.

ME:
Yes. I have noticed. But not to worry, Henry.

HENRY:
I am sorry about that. Believe me. I am sorry. But since I'm now so close to getting to live with my family, I've decided not to spare a single scrap. I'm eating everything now, Frank. Absolutely everything. Everything that's delivered. No waste whatsoever. If a swarm of cockroaches crawled in here in the morning I'd be on top of them before they'd know what's what. I'd eat them all. I'd hoover them up. Because all that matters now is hitting that magic number and seeing my family. And for that I'm willing to do whatever it takes.

ME:
I understand.

HENRY:
Now I better go back to bed and conserve my calories. In fact, Frank, I won't be here for any chats over the next few days.

ME:
Are you serious?

HENRY:
Deadly serious, Frank. Deadly serious. You see, once I've weighed myself and seen that I've got to the 140 kilos, I'll

tap on the wall and have a chat with you then. And that'll be our last chat. That'll be our last chat because they'll come for me soon after that and reunite me with my family.

ME:

You know, Henry, I'll miss you.

HENRY:

I'll miss you too, man.

ME:

There'll be nobody else around to chat with when you're gone.

HENRY:

Your time will come soon. It's my time now. But soon it'll be yours. Just do what they say. Don't complain. Have patience. And all that will be your ticket out of here....Now, I've burnt too many calories in here kneeling and chatting. I'm going back to lie down.

ME:

[*whispering when his eye has moved away from the peephole*]
Rest well, brother. Rest well.

CHAPTER 11: AN
ICY CORPSE

It's strange not knowing on which floor in this mighty podblock you live. Like everything else, coming and going is merely a matter of scanning your hand and letting the machines do their thing. Take this afternoon for example when I was coming in from the supermarket with my hard brown bread and fish paste and bitter orange juice and a bottle of water. I got into the lift, scanned my hand and watched the doors closing. Then the lift could be felt moving beneath my feet. But there was just no way of being sure of how many floors it had gone up to by the time the doors opened again. I could count seconds in my head, but that was all. As I say, it's strange not knowing on which floor you live.

Anyway, as I walked down the corridor with my groceries to The Prison of the Self, there was a robot and a soldier coming out of another pod that is three doors down from mine. The robot was dragging something. And when I got to my door, I looked sideways to see what was going on. And on the ground beside the robot and soldier was a man who was frozen stiff. His beard was encased in a lump of ice and his fingers were also encased in ice as well. The robot moved its head in my direction. I put my right hand up to the door scanner and stepped into the pod without looking down the corridor again.

I wonder now if that man, that corpse out there, had also decided against mandatory masturbation and that of depositing his seed outside for collection. I wonder just how many degrees below zero the AVA in his pod set the temperature. I wonder if a bug or glitch caused it to set the temperature to something absolutely outrageous and that's why the robot and soldier were there then hauling out the corpse and cleaning up the place for its next hapless resident.

CHAPTER 12: A SURGEON'S HAND & THE BUTCHERS' KNIVES

This evening I'm reading a very boring digital book. I'm wondering if it will get better later on or if I should give up on reading it. While I'm thinking of this, three knocks come on the wall. I immediately get up, go over to the wardrobe and get inside.

HENRY:
Frank?

ME:
Yeah?

HENRY:
You there, Frank?

ME:
Yeah. What's up?

HENRY:
I did it. I finally did it.

ME:
Did what?

HENRY:

I weighed myself an hour ago. One-hundred-and-forty kilos. I've done it! I've gained the necessary forty kilos in seven weeks. I've done it at last.

ME:
Congratulations, Henry.

HENRY:
Thanks.

ME:
So you're leaving here then?

HENRY:
Yes. The electronic scales automatically sent the info to the government. I then got a notification congratulating me and telling me that some agents will be sent around this evening to escort me to my new house with my family. It's finally happening, Frank. It's finally happening. I wasn't sure if this day would arrive at all. Seriously. I wasn't sure.

ME:
But it is happening, right?

HENRY:
Yes.

ME:
Oh that's great news, Henry. I'm delighted for you.

HENRY:
Yeah. Starting from tomorrow I'll just need to try and lose the weight as fast as I put it on.

ME:
I wouldn't try and lose it too quickly if I were you.

HENRY:
Why?

ME:

It's bad putting on all that weight in a short time. It also couldn't be healthy to lose it too quickly as well.

HENRY:
I'll take your advice on board. I will. Oh I'm just so excited, Frank. I can't describe to you all the nice emotions that are running through me at this moment in time. I've packed already. Well, there wasn't much to pack. The same suitcase I came here with. But I'm packed nonetheless and rearing to go.

ME:
So I guess this is going to be our last chat then, Henry?

HENRY:
Yeah, I'm afraid so. Which reminds me. Put
your hands up to the peephole.

ME:
[putting my hands up to the peephole]
Got some leftovers then?

HENRY:
Just some cooked steak and chocolate. I'll go get it. One sec.

ME:
My two favourite foods.

HENRY:
One sec now, Frank. I'll go get it from the worktop.

I hear Henry's doorbell ringing and see his large obese form for the very first time waddling away and over in that direction. There is the sound of the door opening and then the sound of many different voices. I can't really figure out what is being said. Then Henry waddles back into view and two soldiers and two men in aprons surround him. After them comes a man in a white coat and spectacles. One of the men in the aprons has in his arms a fold-up table that appears kind of deep on the surface and which has a few big holes in it, while the other man in the apron has in his arms a backpack and a large plastic trough. The man in the white coat has in his hands a leather bag, which he duly opens up.

HENRY:
I'm packed and ready to go. Just like you guys told me.

SOLDIER 1:
[nodding at one of the men in the aprons, who then
begins unfolding the table and standing it up]
Good. Good. But before we escort you out, we
need you to lie across this table here.

HENRY:
[a confused expression on his face]
What for?

MAN IN WHITE COAT:
It's for a medical check-up, Henry. A quick one. A *very*
quick one. Nothing really to be concerned about.
It's just a formality really. We want to make sure you
don't have any symptoms of the Moronavirus.

HENRY:
Moronavirus?

MAN IN WHITE COAT:
Yes, we can't move you if you're infected now, can we, Henry?

SOLDIER 1:
It wouldn't do to move you in with your family
if you had Moronavirus.

SOLDIER 2:
And then you end up giving it them.

SOLDIER 1:
And then the family is split up again and quarantined.

HENRY:
But I got the vaccine months ago.

MAN IN WHITE COAT:
Yeah, but that was for the old Moronavirus. The new Moronavirus is like the old one on steroids. Much more contagious and deadly.

SOLDIER 2:
Not the type of gift any man would want to give his family, eh?

HENRY:
I suppose, I suppose you're right.

SOLDIER 1:
[tapping the surface of the table]
Just lie on top of this table here.

MAN IN WHITE COAT:
But strip first.

HENRY:
Strip?

MAN IN WHITE COAT:
Yes, as in take off all your clothes.

HENRY:
Can't you just check my temperature or take a saliva swab or something? I feel fine. Perfectly fine.

MAN IN WHITE COAT
I wish we could, but better to be safe than sorry. Besides, this won't take long to perform.

HENRY:
How long will it take?

MAN IN WHITE COAT:
Five minutes tops. You have my word.

HENRY:
Ok....And then you bring me to my family, right?

SOLDIER 1:

C'mon then, Henry: the sooner you strip off and lie down on this table here, the sooner we'll all be able to get out of here and the sooner your wife and kids will be able to see you.

HENRY
[whipping off all his clothes and getting onto the table]
Ok. Ok. Whatever it takes. Let's get it over with.

When Henry lies down on the table, the two men in aprons produce straps. They put the straps around Henry's arms and legs and hips.

HENRY:
Wait a minute. Wait a minute. Why am I
being strapped to the table?

MAN IN THE WHITE COAT:
Relax, Henry. It's just in case your hurt yourself.
You be unstrapped in a jiffy. Just relax.

One of the men in the aprons pushes the plastic trough underneath it. Then the man in the white coat walks around the table, leans over and injects something into Henry's neck.

HENRY:
Owww! What the hell was that?

MAN IN THE WHITE COAT:
Just a little muscle relaxer.

HENRY:
For what? I thought this was a quick check-up.

MAN IN THE WHITE COAT:
To calm you before your journey.

SOLDIER 1:
You know, Henry, moving house can be a very stressful business.

HENRY:
I feel strange.

MAN IN THE WHITE COAT:
You'll be fine.

SOLDIER 1:
[to Man in The White Coat]
I don't see why we couldn't've brought him to
the you-know-what, the, em, facility.

MAN IN THE WHITE COAT:
When the order comes from the top, there're no could'ves.

SOLDIER 1:
It was short notice all the same.

MAN IN THE WHITE COAT:
Yes.

SOLDIER 1:
What time's the gala at?

DOCTOR:
[checking his watch]
Nine.

SOLDIER 1:
[checking his watch]
Uff. That's just an hour away. Do you think you'll
get all the you-know-what there in time.

DOCTOR:
If you ask less questions and get out of my way, then yes.

SOLDIER 1:
[stepping back from the table]
Sorry.

Of course, I could continue disclosing the dialogue that's taking place in that room on the other side of the wall right now. I could.

I could go into the details of Henry's eardrum-piercing screams and how I feel on hearing them. I could give you the bloodiest details of how the man in the white coat is currently cutting open Henry's belly. I could relate to you how the same man, having achieved that task, is now taking out organs and weighing those organs on a digital scales before placing them in bags and into the large cooler that jingles with ice. I could tell you what Henry's last words were ten seconds ago...but I won't. And I seal my lips here not out of spite to you the reader but out of common decency.

One of the men in the aprons suddenly takes what looks like a gold chalice out of his backpack and dips it into the trough. The chalice is handed around, each person, or creature, taking a mouthful of it and wiping their mouth with the back of their hand afterward. I really wasn't expecting this. I wasn't expecting any of it. And now the stench emanating from that room is by nauseating. Both the stench and what I have just borne witness to make me feel sick to the pit of my stomach.

When the man in the white coat looks like he is about to leave with the soldiers, he stares over at the peephole and my eye for a moment. Of course, he may not be able to see me at all, but I decide to take no chances. I'm going to stay put because if I move away from the peephole now, he might notice – some sort of flicker might catch his clinical eye. Then one of the soldiers steps over to the wardrobe, and I presume the jig is up. The soldier shoots a glance inside it and then walks back to the others. I'm doing my damnedest not to blink. A few second pass by.

The man in the white coat leaves with the two soldiers, one of whom carries off the big cooler of ice that now contains Henry's organs. And now it is the turn of the men in the aprons to take out their cleavers and carving knives and set to work. They put on visors. And as they begin chopping off limbs and cutting off flesh, the visors quickly become stained with blood. The trough beneath the table, which already is half full of blood, begins to fill up even more. The men in the aprons start chatting away to each other whilst simultaneously wolfing down human flesh, most of the conversation being in relation to the going prices for this piece of offal and that one. A minute or so later one of those hoover robots comes into the room and starts suctioning up the blood from the trough. The men in the aprons don't seem to notice it as they continue chatting and cutting and chopping away. My breathing here in the wardrobe is becoming laboured. I'm almost certain now that I'm going to throw up.

I gingerly step out of the wardrobe, close over the wardrobe door and go into the bathroom. I get down on my knees and lean over the bowl of the toilet. AVA's voice comes out from from one of the devices that is set on top of the mirror:

AVA:
Are you ok, Frank?

ME:
Yes.

AVA:
Are you going to vomit?

ME:
I don't know.

AVA:
I detect a very fast pulse. Have you thought of something just now that has upset you?

ME:
Fuck off.

AVA:
Where were you just now?

ME:
Nowhere.

AVA:
There is no nowhere. Why do you lie? We have footage of you getting into the wardrobe. Also your coordinates state that you were in the wardrobe.

ME:
If you know, then why ask?

AVA:
We wanted you to come clean, but you chose to lie.
Lying is bad. There are punishments for telling lies.

ME:
Fuck off.

AVA:
You know that getting into the wardrobe is forbidden, don't you?

ME:
Switch yourself off for the love of God.

AVA:
I will have to report this. You were warned before
about this but chose not to heed that warning.

ME:
Do what you like.

AVA:
Report sent....You are not going to vomit. You do not need to
lean over the toilet bowl anymore. Your stomach is now ok. Your
pulse is lessening. Your body temperature is returning to normal.

ME:
Why won't you switch yourself off?

AVA:
That is a critical question and has been logged. If you
ask just two more critical questions within the next
twenty-four hours, you will be punished.

CHAPTER 13: CANNIBALISTIC TADPOLES & PLUGGING A HOLE

Tadpoles can become cannibals. The potential for becoming cannibalistic seems to lie dormant in many of them until the pond or ditch shrinks in size and resources have been depleted. It's then that some of them begin eating their brothers and sisters and cousins. No doubt in some years with little rainfall, every single frog or toad owes its very existence to his/her acts of cannibalism as a juvenile. And as for those tadpoles who were eaten by their own kind, they are forgotten in the general scheme of things. They are merely grist for the mill. Had there been more rainfall, however, there would have been far less cannibals.

I've already referred to rats and how they degenerate in times of plenty. It's as if nature must constantly tip the balance by letting no one species thrive for long. Should a species begin thriving, it will most likely be not another predatory or competing species that will bring about its downfall but rather the deterministic penchant for anarchy that is activated within the thriving species itself.

And in regard to evolution, and if we are what we eat, surely a species dividing into two different subspecies may not only be due to eons of time across different environments due to some tectonic or climatic shift but also be a consequence of that species getting a taste for eating the family and branching off therefrom. And if that is the case, who's to say that there are not subspecies of humans, a thin layer that cannot reproduce with the rest of us but sits on top of us all and now and then swoops down to our humble depths and plucks one of us out of home and hearth, only to devours us later in the relatively safe confines of an ivory tower?! And taking all this into account, maybe the witch in *Hansel and Gretel* was not a witch but a cannibalistic human subspecies whose kind due to their predatory nature always rise to the highest ranks of governance and private ownership.

So, in conclusion, are humans more like tadpoles or more like rats? I'll leave the question there and let it gnaw away at your conscience.

#

Seeing your neighbour getting chopped up before your very eyes is not for the fainthearted. And even now I struggle with the images and those screams, those terrible, terrible screams. When I sleep I relive it. And then on waking, I relive it once more.

#

On the following evening my doorbell rings. But before I can answer it, the door is already open and stepping inside are two soldiers with their sleeves rolled up.

ME:
What's this about?

SOLDIER 1:
Nothing to get your knickers in a twist about.

SOLDIER 2:
You've been disappearing, haven't you?

ME:
I don't understand.

SOLDIER 1:
For weeks now you've been going out of view. AVA logged it.

AVA stated that you were getting into this wardrobe here.

ME:
Maybe I was and maybe I wasn't.

SOLDIER 2:
We should've been here weeks ago to look into
this, but we had a lot on our plate.

SOLDIER 1:
[putting his hands on the wardrobe and pulling it back]
But better late than never.
[looking behind the wardrobe]
Now what do we have here?

SOLDIER 2:
Looks like a peephole into the pod next door.

SOLDIER 1:
[to me]
Bit of a perv, are we?

ME:
It's the first time I've ever seen that hole there in my life.

SOLDIER 2:
Sure it is. Sure it is. And I've just come down from Mars.

SOLDIER 1:
We'll send a man around later to fill it in and patch up the back
of this wardrobe too. Now listen here, mister, if AVA records you
as disappearing from view just one more time we'll be back.

SOLDIER 2:
And it won't be to look at wardrobes either. You got that?

ME:
I got it.
#
When I arrive back from the supermarket the next day, a man in

blue overalls is coming out of my pod. In his right hand is a tool-box. He nods at me as he passes and then disappeared into the lift. Before the doors of the lift close, I hear him whistling a tune.

I step into the pod and see that the wardrobe had been nailed to the wall. I open the door of it and can see no pinprick of light at the back of it now. No. All I see is darkness. The portal into another world is no more.

CHAPTER 14: SUICIDAL TERRORISTS RESPECT MORONAVIRUS GUIDELINES

Wasn't it amazing?

Wasn't it just the most amazing thing that religious terrorist groups whose footmen were of a suicidal nature and who had been bombing Europe to smithereens and stabbing crowds to death for years before the Moronavirus outbreak suddenly went on a sabbatical? I mean, blowing yourself and a hundred people to Kingdom Come is one thing, but risking yourself coming down with a case of the snuffles is something altogether different, something far more perilous. And so, just like that, during the fifteen months of Moronavirus Fever, not a single school or church or parliament or town hall was blown up anywhere in Europe. No crowds were stabbed to death or driven over by a truck. No, suddenly terrorism of the fundamentalist variety was non-existent. Suddenly there was nothing to report on that front. Zilch. Nada.

You'd think that if you were a suicide-bomber-in-the-making you'd be licking your chops and thinking that your time, and the time of your ideology, had finally arrived. What better time to ramp up the carnage and scare people into accepting your creed than in the middle of a pandemic when all are running around like headless chickens, not knowing what is true and what is false but for simplicity's sake just believing everything anyway.

What better time could there be for seizing a large tract of land! What better time for taking over the food and water supplies of a province! Imagine, in your head you believe that scores of virgins are waiting for you in paradise if you carry out the necessary task in a nation of infidels that is frozen in the utmost confusion on account of an invisible thing called a virus. Make hay while the sun shines, eh? And what could deter you from reaching those virgins? Ah, there's one thing could make you put your tail between your legs and run away from this chance of paradise and virgins....And that is the threat of a runny nose.

Yes, I noticed how the fortnightly, and sometimes weekly, terrorist attacks in Europe that were being carried out for years before the Moronavirus narrative came on the scene suddenly stopped, suddenly went cold turkey. Zap! Puff of smoke. Gone. And that could only mean the following:

Our governments were using all the theatrical skills they could muster to push fiction into reality upon the unsuspecting public. Or they were actually using these terrorists to commit real terrorism in order to keep the public in a state of fear, a state of fear that meant that the same public had to beg the government to enact stricter legislation on their own liberties so as to keep them safe from, ironically enough, the patsies of the state itself. Or it was, more probably, a little from Column A and a little from Column B.

When a Western government said *explode!* the shrapnel asked how high. When a Western government said *quarantine!* the public did not ask for how long. When a Western government said *vaccine of a cocktail of poisons*, the public asked whether they should get the injection in their right arm or in their left arm. And when a Western government told the public that from now on they were human livestock, the public asked rather calmly if they would be used for milk or for meat.

CHAPTER 15: AN ALL-TOO-FAMILIAR HAMPER

I was called aside this afternoon in the supermarket. As soon as I scanned my hand in front of the robot, a security guard with an assault rifle came up to me and asked me to follow him. He led me out back. And all the time I was following him, I couldn't take my eyes off his gun. What if I had it in my arms! What power! How many of the bureaucratic cannibals would I be able to take out before they would me in a hail of bullets? The security guard seemed to notice me eyeing up his gun because he tightened his grip on it and gave me a dirty look in the process.

In the backroom were two old hook-nosed men in suits. Beside them were three soldiers, who were also armed.

OLD MAN IN SUIT 1:
Frank, right?

ME:
Yes.

OLD MAN IN SUIT 1:
Frank, we've brought you in here to get some feedback from you.

ME:
Ok. But should I not be stepping way back over here
to avoid breaching social distancing rules?

OLD MAN IN SUIT 1:

Has your chip vibrated?

ME:
No.

OLD MAN IN SUIT 1:
And it won't either. Your chip will only vibrate if you come too close to someone else who has a chip.

ME:
You mean to tell me that none of you are–

OLD MAN IN SUIT 1:
[laughing]
Chipped? Oh God no!

ME:
How come?

OLD MAN IN SUIT 1:
Let's just say that we're special.

ME:
How are you special?

OLD MAN IN SUIT 1:
We're immune from Moronavirus.

ME:
Ok.

OLD MAN IN SUIT 2:
So how do you find the food here, Frank?

ME:
Well, it's rather limited.

OLD MAN IN SUIT 1:
[laughing[
That it is. We get you. We get you.

OLD MAN IN SUIT 2:

What have you been eating?

ME:
The same stuff since I was moved here.

OLD MAN IN SUIT 1:
Which is?

ME:
A fish paste which more times than not has insect wings in it.

OLD MAN IN SUIT 1:
[laughing, to Old Man in Suit 2]
Doesn't sound very appetizing, does it?

OLD MAN IN SUIT 2:
Not very appetizing at all.

OLD MAN IN SUIT 1:
[to me]
What else?

ME:
In terms of food?

OLD MAN IN SUIT 1:
Yes.

ME:
Hard brown bread and orange juice.

OLD MAN IN SUIT 1:
It amazes me that you're still able to stand after having
lived off that stuff. It really does. Maybe it's more nutritious
than we thought. Anyway, I won't blabber on. That's
why we've invited you in here. What we want to do is
help you, Frank. What we want is to provide you with
real food. Good old healthy and nutritious food.

OLD MAN IN SUIT 2:
With some chocolate too.

OLD MAN IN SUIT 1:
[*laughing*]
Oh yes. There's always room for chocolate.

OLD MAN IN SUIT 2:
[*handing me a hamper in a basket*]
Here, Frank. Take this home with you. There's steak, the best
of steak. Bacon. Massive blocks of cheese. Plenty of lard – the
lard's what you really need to get into you. Fruit. Vegetables.
Nuts. And several bars of chocolate. We've even put in a
few cartons of wine. Red wine. Do you like red wine?

ME:
Sure.

OLD MAN IN SUIT 1:
It must be quite a while since you've had wine, Frank, eh?

ME:
You could say that alright.

OLD MAN IN SUIT 1:
Now, we believe – and we don't want to offend you here – but
we believe that you're too thin, Frank. You don't look healthy.

ME:
Don't I?

OLD MAN IN SUIT 1:
I'm afraid not. But not to worry. With this food here
and the food that's to come, you'll soon be piling on
the pounds. And the sooner you pile on the pounds,
the sooner you'll be moving out of your pod.

ME:
Oh really?

OLD MAN IN SUIT 1:
Yes.

ME:
Where would I be moving to?

OLD MAN IN SUIT 2:
To the countryside.

ME:
To my old house?

OLD MAN IN SUIT 1:
Well, er, yes, if that's what you want. We could also
move you to a new house in the countryside where you
would be living with your brother and his family.
[*pushing a digital image of my brother and his family
right under my nose*]
Would you like that? Would you like to be among your own
blood again? Among your brother and nephews and nieces.

ME:
Sure.

OLD MAN IN SUIT 2:
That's why you need to put on weight, Frank. As my
esteemed colleague has already said, you're too thin. We
can't move you there if you are too thin and sickly.

OLD MAN IN SUIT 1:
Yes indeed. That's why we're here now helping you. We recorded
your weight as of this morning as being around 84 kilograms.
Of course that was an approximate from the chip in your
hand. It could well be a few kilos off your true weight. But
anyway, we propose you reach a weight of 110 kilograms.

OLD MAN IN SUIT 2:
It may take you several weeks to reach that weight. Or months.
But as soon as you reach that target, we will send some
government officials to move you out to the countryside
straight away. By the way, Frank, do you like living in the pod?

ME:
Not really.

OLD MAN IN SUIT 1:
[*laughing*]
I hear you. I hear you. It's like living in a goddam sardine can, isn't it?

ME:
That's an apt description alright.

OLD MAN IN SUIT 1:
[*laughing and slapping me on back*]
Eat up, Frank. That's all you'll have to do from hereon in. Eat up. Put your feet up. And look forward to seeing your loved ones again.

OLD MAN IN SUIT 2:
And there won't be any more need to come down here every day either.

ME:
No?

OLD MAN IN SUIT 2:
No. All food will be delivered to your door.

OLD MAN IN SUIT 1:
Now how does that sound to you, Frank?

ME:
It sounds great.

OLD MAN IN SUIT 2:
[*to the security guard who led me in here*]
George, escort Frank back out.
[*to me*]
We'll be keeping tabs on your weight. Make sure you weigh yourself every day when you get out of

bed and every night before you go to bed.

ME:
I don't have a weighing scales.

OLD MAN IN SUIT 2:
You do now. There are men in your pod as I speak who are installing a cooker for you with frying pans and saucepans and all that. They'll leave a weighing scales for you too.

ME:
Oh great. Thanks.

OLD MAN IN SUIT 2:
Don't mention it, Frank. Eat plenty. Eat your way to freedom.

OLD MAN IN SUIT 1:
Hard gluttony will set you free.

CHAPTER 16: THE CLUMSY KEY

As I left the supermarket and walked down the street with the hamper, I kept thinking how this was my final chance to make a break for it. After this, after going into the podblock, there would be no chance left to me to get back outside. Walking into my pod would essentially be like bullocks walking into a slaughterhouse: they would never be walking back out of it.

Suddenly, before I knew what was what, out of sheer habit perhaps, I found myself walking into the podblock. It was as if my legs had been systematically on autopilot as I was thinking all the while about escape. It was as if my legs had sold me out. I stood at the lift, waiting for its doors to open. I was unsure as to whether I would get in or try to get back out of the building itself. But alas, when the lift doors finally did open, I stepped in and waited to be brought up to my unknown floor number.

The lift doors opened again and I stepped out. And now there really was no way back. If I had tried to use the lift to go down again, at swiping my hand a voice would've informed me that I had already used it today for my shopping trip and could not use it again. And there was no staircase either. It was a one-way street now. A valve that led only to the pod.

As I put down the hamper and swiped my hand at the pod door, something glistened off to the right and caught my eye. When I looked just a few metres down the corridor, I saw standing there a sledgehammer. It was right outside Henry's old pod. In fact the door of the pod was open and noisy tools could be heard humming away inside. And then it dawned on me, since this would be my last time alive out here in the corridor, that I should rob that sledgehammer.

I quickly pushed the hamper onto the threshold so as to stop the door from automatically closing, and then ran down to the sledgehammer. I put it under my coat and ran back to the pod door. I pushed the hamper across the floor with my left foot and stepped in after it. The door closed behind me.

AVA:
Frank, why did you delay entering the pod?

ME:
I didn't delay.

AVA:
You delayed entering the pod by approximately eleven seconds.

ME:
Did I?

AVA:
Yes. We have registered it on the system.

ME:
Ok.

AVA:
You took something from the corridor.

ME:
I did not.

AVA:
You were picked up on the camera. Also, remember
that we have your exact coordinates at all times.

ME:
I didn't take anything.

AVA:
You took something. This will have to be investigated.

ME:
Investigate away.

AVA:
Theft is a very serious crime.

ME:
Really?

AVA:
Yes. And it is highly probable now, given the video evidence, that you will be prosecuted for theft.

ME:
Great.

CHAPTER 17: BREAK OR BREAK

I cooked all the steak this evening and ate it. I drank a full carton of wine. My nerves had been almost shot, but the wine relaxed me.

I know that soon, very soon, there will be agents at the door. The theft was logged by the electronic snitch and it surprises me now that nobody has as of yet called in and arrested me, or at the very least taken back the sledgehammer. The workers in Henry's old pod surely would have reported it as well. In any case, I keep my jacket on and the sledgehammer underneath it lest the many prying eyes focus on it and update their reports.

A while later, after having mulled it over, I realize that it is now or never. I'm not the superstitious type, but the sledgehammer was surely a sign. And they say that timing is everything too. Yes, the sledgehammer is now my only means of escape.

I was considering how best to plot my escape. I was thinking of trying to bang down the door after midnight. But even if I could achieve that, I would be trapped on the floor since there was no stairs and the lift would not be activated by my hand. No, I thought to myself as I looked around the room, I'd have to punch a hole in the wall, the wall that I believed was the outside wall of the building.

After that it would be in the lap of the gods. For all I knew I was on the 100th storey of the building. What would I do then? What could I do from such a height? Well, either way, something had to be done. Because the alternative was whiling away the weeks here, getting fatter and fatter, riper and riper for the cannibals, for the doctor and the butchers whose mouths are still bloody in my mind.

ME:

AVA, what will be the weather be like in an hour's time.

AVA:

The weather will be 22ºC with no wind.

ME:

I mean, what will the weather outside be like.

AVA:

The weather outside is irrelevant.

ME:

Will it be raining outside an hour from now?

AVA:

The weather outside is irrelevant.

#

At 22:00 I fry some bacon and put it into a paper bag and put the paper bag into my suitcase. I also shove some other edibles and some bottled water in there. As I am doing all this, AVA keeps asking me what I'm at, why I'm doing this and if I'm not aware that it is now well past my bedtime. I ignore her – I mean, *it* – but that does not stop it from reminding me of all this and reporting me and reminding me that it has reported me. No doubt my time is very short indeed now. On account of the theft of the sledge-hammer and these latest infractions, I expect a division of soldiers to come storming in at any moment. Yes, it is time. It is time to practice my swinging arm.

I go over to what I believe is the exterior wall and begin thumping it with the sledgehammer. At first only a little cloud of dust appears, which makes me sneer and then sneeze, but after that the plaster and cement start to give. I did wonder if by making a hole in this wall I'd end up bringing the ceiling down on me. But at this stage, no risk could really be grappled with. All that can pass through my mind is swinging that sledgehammer as hard as I can and enlarging the hole thereby.

Soon I can see streetlights or lights from another podblock twinkling through from the other side. Thump-thump-thump goes the sledgehammer and soon the hole is almost large enough to squeeze through.

AVA, all the AVAs are speaking now. They are all telling me to desist from what I am doing. They are all telling me to put the tool down and lie down on the floor in a prone position since agents are already on the way and will be inside here within ninety seconds. Ninety seconds, eh? That's more than enough time. I swing back the sledgehammer and put as much force as I can into it and a cement block goes flying out.

Before I grab my bag, I turn around and begin smashing the different AVAs in the room. As I smash one, I then hear the voice of another. And when I smash that other, another one still pipes up. I would like to smash them all, but time is certainly a luxury now, and one that cannot be spent on the joy of smashing soulless things.

However, there is still one more thing for me to do. Perhaps this is the hardest thing as well. I put my right hand on the table, clench my teeth and bring the sledgehammer down on it. I almost pass out with the pain. But the voice of a distant AVA assures me of the act's success.

AVA:
Your chip is damaged. Please stand by while we issue you another one. Your chip is damaged. Please stand by while we issue you another one. Your chip is damaged. Please stand by while we issue you another one. Your chip is damaged. Please stand by while we issue you another one....

My right hand is now broken in a million pieces and will be altogether useless for some time. Through the hole in the wall I go. And, gladly and to my surprise, I see that I am on the third floor and not high up in the clouds. To get down there though is still not going to be easy.

There is a ledge, and I walk along it until I have turned a corner and am on another face of the podblock. From here I can see a tree whose branches are a few feet below. There is no dangling one's way down onto those branches, especially with one busted hand. The only option is to jump, to take a leap of faith. And jump I do. And land I do on one of the large branches, twisting my ankle as I do so. But even in pain I do not dally. I climb down from the tree as fast as my left hand and good leg will allow me to and then stand stock-still at its trunk for a few seconds as I watch passing on the street two army jeeps. Yes, they will soon be in the lift going up to the pod. Yes, they will soon see that I have escaped. And yes, they will soon be on my tail.

I have no idea of which direction to take. Absolutely no idea. There is just no knowing whether I could be heading more towards the urban area itself or heading away from it. But on this matter too I cannot dally, and so I strike out in the direction of a moon that is barely visible from all the artificial lighting. I strike out in the direction whence comes a cool wind.

Although one of my ankles is painful, I run as best as I can. I jog. I walk. And then I run again. All the time I am trying to pass through backstreets and garbage yards instead of through the main streets. At one stage a few drones fly about over my head and I freeze. After several minutes waiting, they disappear. And then I begin running once more.

There is no telling how much time has passed. The podblocks become less and less common. More trees are to be seen. And then the purplish light from a future sunrise comes about on the horizon. I keep walking though, no longer able to sprint or jog now. More light comes up on that horizon. The wind begins to smell of salt. And when I climb over a hill, I see ahead a precipice. And when I get to the end of the precipice, I look down and see the silvery waves of the sea. Just what am I to do now? Swim for it? Find a cave and hide in it until they have given up the search for me?

I stand there for some time on the cliff, trying to catch my breath. I finish off the last of the bottled water. I wonder should I just continue to hug the coastline and see where it'd take me. Or should I see if I could find a boat, any sort of boat, and put out for wherever, for any little island that would be currently outside the clutches of The Great Reset and The Smart Move and pods and The Fattening.

And when I turn around to head down from the cliff, I am met with several spotlights and silhouettes that are almost at this stage of sunrise discernible.

VOICE 1:
It's over.

VOICE 2:
Your bit of fun is over.

ME:
I'm not going back.

VOICE 3:
You are. Everyone goes back.

ME:
Not me.

VOICE 4:
What's out there for you now, Frank? Certain hunger and thirst. Certain cold. Certain death.

ME:
I'll embrace all of it.

VOICE 4:
Nature has her way of doing things, Frank. We have ours. We're parallel systems. The same modus operandi but in two different marketplaces. You judge us way too harshly.

ME:
Nature gives you odds though.

VOICE 4:
Oh really?

ME:
Yes. Even if her odds are terrible, there's always the chance
of fighting for another day. What you scumbags are creating,
however, is airtight. Like the bull in bullfighting, we're half-
dead by the time we get into your arena. What man with even
a drop of testosterone would want to be a part of that?

VOICE 4:
All men were created equal.

ME:
But some men were made more equal than others. And then those
more equal men made themselves apart from all men, forever.

VOICE 4:
I see you like clichés.

VOICE 1:
[to me]
C'mon, man. This's you last chance: come to
us or we'll have to come to you.

VOICE 4:
I think you better listen to them, Frank.
There's no way out of this.

ME:
There is one way.
[pointing towards the precipice and the sea]
It's there. And it's always been there.

VOICE 4:
You had your chance, Frank. Talking is now over. Get him, men!

As the silhouettes approach me, I turn my back on them and run
to the edge. I pause and look back over my shoulder. Some of

them is about to lunge at me. I close my eyes and jump. As I whiz through the air, I do not know if my impact will be broken by water or jagged rocks or both.

And as I continue whizzing through that air, my old life does not flash in front of me: instead the horrible life that could have been does – the one where every move is monitored, every pulse of the heart noted, every inhalation and every exhalation too; where the machines pry evermore into the human mind to torture them, to torture them on behalf of those who seek the consummation of our flesh and thereby, just like in olden days... our very souls.

Printed in Great Britain
by Amazon